HIGH VISTA

To Jane & John

Best Wishes

Sabe Thomas.

HIGH VISTA

SALIE THOMAS

Matador
Unit E2 Airfield Business Park,
Harrison Road, Market Harborough,
Leicestershire. LE16 7UL
Tel: 0116 2792299
Email: books@troubador.co.uk
Web: www.troubador.co.uk/matador
Twitter: @matadorbooks

ISBN 978-1-80514-219-5

British Library Cataloguing in Publication Data.
A catalogue record for this book is available from the British Library.

Printed and bound in Great Britain by 4edge Limited
Typeset in 10.5pt Garamond Pro by Troubador Publishing Ltd, Leicester, UK

Matador is an imprint of Troubador Publishing Ltd

Many thanks to my friend Wendy Robertson
for taking me to Spain.

ONE

For twelve years the Jensen and Son sign had lit up the entrance to the office and yard on the outskirts of Luton.

The Jensens had worked together as a family to build a highly profitable construction business and Jimmy, their eldest son, was made a partner for his fortieth birthday.

Teddy and Joanna had three children: James, Brian and Suzanna. James (Jimmy) had always been keen to join the company and had qualified as a quantity surveyor. Brian was different: he liked the high life in London and chose to go into insurance, and with a hobby of dealing with high class cars he soon bought a flat in Hammersmith and another flat in Earls Field well before the prices went up. Then there was Suzanna, who could have been a film star, top fashion model or anything she fancied, but as long as she could go abroad, stay in top hotels and dine out at luxury restaurants she was happy. Teddy and Jo were very pleased when she met, fell in love with and married Alan Jones when she was twenty one. She also continued to work in the office while Alan finished his uni course.

Teddy and Jo were devastated when in February their beloved son Jimmy was killed on his way home from work in an accident on the M1. There was a massive pile-up with ten vehicles involved.

Teddy was about to hand over the business to Jimmy and was looking forward to retirement. Everything seemed to change from that day.

The business had become a drag; the enthusiasm had died with Jimmy and fulfilling the contracts was just laborious, so when a Canadian conglomerate wanted to extend their business into Britain and needed a base near London it was a great relief to sell the whole lot to them for a cool fifty million pounds.

Teddy had agreed to stay on for a year to ease the new people into their English enterprise. Suzannah and Alan took on a chateau in France, and Teddy and Jo badly needed a holiday somewhere warm and sunny.

Their close friends, George and Gail Brown, owned an apartment in the centre of Fuengirola, Spain, that sounded ideal as it was near enough for Teddy to return if he was needed.

TWO

In early September, after a comfortable flight from London leaving heavy rain and thunder behind, Teddy and Jo arrived at the apartment in Fuengirola. A small Spanish woman of about fifty opened the door and welcomed them in.

"I'm Sharda, I come once a week," she said. She cleaned and put fresh fruit in a big bowl on the dining room table and then showed them into the kitchen where she had put fresh bread, milk and coffee and various meats. "Now I go, be back on Friday," she said with a smile and was gone.

The apartment looked comfortable and ample for a holiday home. The master bedroom had an ensuite, a small balcony and lots of cupboard space. The second bedroom had two single beds and a shower room across the passage. The sitting room had a spacious balcony overlooking a large garden with a swimming pool and lovely palm trees for shade. The scent of mock orange and different herbs hung everywhere.

"A month here will do us the world of good," Teddy mused as they sat in the shade of the balcony sipping the champagne Jo had found in the fridge with a card from George and Gail welcoming them.

The next two weeks were spent exploring the shops, cafes and area in and around Fuengirola. Their favourite being the marina: with a diverse choice of food from Spanish, French, German, Danish and English while looking at the fantastic yachts and boats.

On a keyring in the kitchen there was a label saying, 'garage no. eight, please leave the car full of fuel'. No.8 was near the end of a row of lockups and inside was a smart red Seat ready to go. Their plan was to explore the surrounding areas, towns and villages beginning with Benalmadena, Mehas and a day trip to Gibraltar and just wandering around.

It was on one of those days with no plan that they found a small meandering road going up a mountainside. Eventually they came to a rusty gate with an equally rusty sign saying, 'High Vista'. "Let's go up," Teddy laughed and on they went.

They reached the top, which opened out into quite a wide area. A concrete mixer and tools were on the side with the best view of the rooftops and then the sea. Fuengirola was about five miles to the right. There was a telescope looking out over the sea, and in the distance was a ferry boat and a sleek catamaran. The buildings were no more than shacks but someone had begun a new building which looked interesting, and a new entrance lower down the hill. There was a newly built stone wall and what looked like a swimming pool under construction.

"Someone is going to have a fabulous home here," Teddy said.

THREE

As they walked around a Jeep drove in and parked next to the Seat. A suntanned older man came towards them. "Yes." He looked hard at them. "This is private land," he said. After apologies and introductions they found that Justin Wright lived in Derbyshire and had bought High Vista two years ago with plans to turn the place into a luxurious holiday home. He had gone through all the legal channels, had everything passed and secure, engaged a local builder and all was progressing well until the day of the storm.

Justin had decided that he needed to go to the barbers and intended to nip out for about an hour. His wife, Rose, was sunning herself while reading a book.

As Justin drove off he noticed dark clouds in the distance but thought nothing of it. The storm broke overhead while Justin was in the barbers. People rushed in from the street for shelter and for five minutes there was utter turmoil. Then as quickly as it arrived the storm passed over and apart from everywhere being soaked and rainwater bubbling up from the drains, normality returned.

Justin noticed a plume of thick smoke over the distant

hilltop and hoped that it was not at High Vista, so he headed back.

There was a group of people, a fire tender and an ambulance. He found paramedics looking after Rose and found out that she had been found on the ground by the deck chair. They assumed that she had been scared when the lightning had struck, fell over hitting her face on the rough ground and was knocked out. After a few hours in hospital she was allowed home, but was too frightened to go back to High Vista so Justin booked them into a hotel until he could get a flight back home to England.

"I'm back here now to put it into the hands of an agent as Rose will never come back."

Teddy and Jo bought High Vista with all its contents for a quick sale for thirty thousand pounds sterling.

The local builders were re-employed and work carried on. The pool was finished first as Teddy said they already had a place to stay in Fuengirola and Jo loved to swim every day.

The main room was very large and partly carved out of rock with a balcony built out overlooking a valley of olive trees and another hill in the distance with apartments and houses looking back to High Vista. The balcony was not finished and was open with girders sticking out over the edge of the mountain, but would look fabulous when completed.

Ginger and Rhanan Jones, Suzannah's in-laws, called to see them and were most impressed.

"You can stay at any time when the guest rooms are ready, which should be quite soon," Teddy said.

Everything continued slowly, with Teddy and Jo doing jobs when the Spanish builders had siesta or turned up late.

While Jo was having her morning swim, Teddy went to get some pipes needed for the kitchen and bathrooms. It was a lovely morning as he waved to her.

Later Jo saw two burly men walk up to the poolside. She felt uneasy but asked if she could be of help. She reached for her towel but was grabbed hard by both men. All they said was, "You were warned." Jo could do nothing as they carried her over to the unfinished balcony. She screamed as they flung her over the edge.

A Spanish woman in one of the apartments was looking through her binoculars and saw everything. She shouted to her husband to come and see the figure of a woman caught by a scrub tree on the edge of the big drop. They called the Guardia who responded immediately, but it took over an hour to get mountain rescuers, doctors and the air ambulance to the scene, but from then on the rescue went smoothly as Jo, still unconscious, was airlifted to hospital.

Teddy had ordered the copper pipes and accessories and then went to their favourite coffee bar where the barman, Jose, was always chatty. He had no idea about the mayhem at High Vista until two policemen came in for a coffee break. Although Teddy did not understand their conversation, he did catch the name, High Vista.

He found out that one of the policemen was from London but had lived in Spain for over twenty years. His name was Johny Bellman and told Teddy about the events and that he should go to the hospital as his wife was very poorly.

Jo was unrecognisable. She had a broken cheekbone and a large cut from her eyebrow to the top of her head, her right shoulder was dislocated and her right wrist was broken. She had three broken ribs and was bruised from head to toe, but was lucky to be alive.

The police had one statement from the Spanish apartment holders and others who saw the two men leaving in a hurry away from High Vista. They were traced to the marina at Bela Madina, then nothing could be followed-up as yet.

The next week was very worrying for Teddy with Jo in intensive care, but because she was so fit with swimming she began to get better and although still very bruised she was able to tell the story to the police. The next two months were spent recovering.

FOUR

Johnny Bellman called to see them most days and he and his family became close friends. The boys, Blake and Ben, loved to swim in the High Vista pool and Jo enjoyed swimming with them. In a way it made her feel safer, and she was only too pleased to give coffee and cake to Johnny and his partner, Philippo, when they had their morning break and chat.

George and Gail sold their red Seat to Jo, and Teddy and Jo moved into High Vista, finished off the decorating and made a comfortable home. All the family had visited and Jo slowly put all her nightmares behind her.

George and Gail had bought a yacht called *Deva Rose* and were enjoying sailing in the Med. When they came back to Spain they invited Teddy and Jo to have a week's holiday with them around Spain.

George used to be the captain of an oil tanker going all over the world and had many stories to tell.

They decided to have lunch at the Fuengirola marina before starting on board for Gibraltar. Johnny and his family had lunch with them and they were surprised when Ginger and Rhanan Jones turned up.

"We were on our way to High Vista," Ginger said. "You invited us to come any time, so here we are."

"Well, that's fine," Jo said. "But we are off on holiday with George and Gail. But you can stay at High Vista and we will be back in a week."

She gave them the keys and showed them where the Seat was parked.

"You will have to buy fresh food as I emptied the fridge, but the freezer is full so help yourself to anything, and use any bedroom as they are all made up."

Ginger and Gail waved them off as George, Gail, Teddy and Jo left the marina heading down the coast to Gibraltar. Lovely weather, calm sea with a slight wind and interesting chat was so relaxing after all the upset and hard work of the last few months. They took plenty of time to explore Gibraltar and Per De Nousem then had two days out at sea fishing, playing cards and listening to George's funny stories about his travels.

Their plan was to sail up the coast then back to Benalmadena, spend the day there then back to Fuengirola, but things changed unexpectedly.

They had a light breakfast on board while looking at the lovely boats in the Bela Madina marina. George had made an appointment to view two apartments with an agent at 11am and Teddy and Jo went with them, which was interesting.

Both apartments were very good to let and could bring in a good income. By 1pm they chose a cafe and ordered lunch during which time Gail noticed people looking at them. Then there were two policemen looking at Teddy and Jo. "Oh, I suppose they read the papers about Jo being thrown over the cliff so just ignore them." Teddy said. Then the two police came over and asked their names. Then there was a lot of Spanish that was not understood but from the tone of their voices they were not happy. One of them went to the paper rack and pulled a paper from it.

"Look," he said, and there on the front page was a picture of Teddy and Jo with headlines which could only mean murdered. The next thing they were being handcuffed and led away to the local police station.

It turned out that two bodies had been found shot and then set alight in bed at High Vista. The red Seat was there and it was assumed that the bodies were Teddy and Jo, hence the newspaper headlines. The police now thought that Teddy and Jo must have killed them and until proved otherwise they had to be in custody.

"Oh dear God, not Ginger and Rhanan," Jo said.

They at last had someone to speak English and when George explained that they had all been together all the time on the yacht since the lunch at Fuengirola when they had left Ginger and Rhanan who were going to stay at High Vista. They also said to ask Johnny Bellman who was with them.

They were eventually released under caution and told to stay in Fuengirola.

Eventually the bodies of Ginger and Rhanan were released and taken to Wales for burial.

FIVE

Teddy was very apprehensive about High Vista after talking to Justin Wright as he found out that it was not the storm that frightened his wife, Rose, but that two strange men had threatened her, then knocked her out. The message was very clear – 'Get Out'.

The place had been empty for about four years and had been used to send messages out to sea when it was safe for drugs to be landed. The police were slowly putting the story together but still could not be sure who were the people responsible. In the meantime, Teddy and Jo moved back into the Fuengirola apartment at night to sleep.

They noticed that people were coming to look around at High Vista every day. A young couple asked if they could open a restaurant there as it was now a famous place.

A two year lease was agreed and Guido and Cloe Garcia took over. They already had a house close to High Vista so the whole place was made into dining areas, a bar and a large kitchen. They had a grand opening and the restaurant was a great success.

Jo had a big birthday coming up: *seventy* in April. They had been in Spain for two eventful years and now their lives seemed settled, their trips back to England became less and Jo was fit again. She decided to have a party at High Vista and invited friends and family from England and France as well as all their new Spanish friends.

The party was a great success and the local press had a full page of all the guests enjoying themselves. The place looked so pretty with twinkling lights everywhere and the pool all in colour.

A surprise was that the pool was named 'Jo's Pool' and the bar was named 'Teddy's Bar', and another brass plaque was in memory of Ginger and Rhanan Jones.

Teddy bought the adjoining apartment to the one George owned and friends could still use George's when it was free.

Life had become really good. They joined a chess club, a book club, a dining club and a monthly excursion group and Jo still found time to swim at least once a day.

SIX

Jo liked to do a weekly shop between eight and nine am every Friday. The local supermarket had everything they needed and the stall holders were always helpful in the market hall. She left with two full bags of groceries and turned past the big bins on the right, when two very attractive young girls came towards her smiling. "Allo," they said, then Jo felt a sharp sting on her left arm.

There seemed to be much laughter and chatting, but Jo could not remember why she was sitting in a wheelchair. Her arms were fastened to the chair arms and her mouth was stuck to with duct tape so she could only make a grunting sound, to which she was told to shut up and had a vicious kick on her shin.

She had sunglasses on and a fancy shawl across her face as they headed for the marina. A large man was pushing her and one of her shopping bags was on her knee. Johnny and Phillipo were walking towards them. Jo made some noises and knocked the bag off her knee, but she was hidden by a large woman pretending to be jolly while picking up the bag. "Do that again and you're dead," the man said quietly while laughing in her ear, making it all look natural.

They lifted her onto a sleek tender, and they were away to a beautiful big catamaran. She noticed the name *Francina Marais.*

"Put her down below," a man said. "We'll deal with her when we get out to sea."

The small room was quite dark with one porthole. There were coats, boots, boxes of wine and scotch, and a big box of flares along with boxes of tinned food.

Jo knew she had to escape somehow and quickly. She leaned forward and pulled the tape off her mouth, then with her teeth she found the end of the tape on her wrist and pulled hard until it lifted up enough for her to release her left arm. At last she was out of the chair.

The porthole was easily opened but had a centre swivel so no room to get through and the door was locked. She was still a prisoner, but what could she do with the flares?

She took as many as she could hold out of the box and read the instructions. *To activate pull the red cord, face it upward at arm's length.*

It was difficult through the porthole and the flair travelled about twenty feet before going into the water. The second one went better. At least it could be seen from the distant shore, but also on deck.

It was not long before she heard someone unlocking the door. She kicked the wheelchair towards the door as a distraction and pulled the red cord. The big man was hit in the throat and fell backwards without saying a word.

Jo set off three more flares into the coats and boxes and then ran along the passage towards the back of the boat. She had two more flares and sent them up as soon as she reached the upper deck, then she jumped overboard and swam hard away from the catamaran. She was free but far from safe. She just kept swimming towards the distant shoreline.

A speedboat was heading near to when there was a really loud bang in the distance, then two more boats were getting closer. Jo was beginning to get tired, then more boats appeared and suddenly someone spotted her. She was lifted onto a small yellow sailing dinghy and given a warm blanket, then she blacked out with exhaustion.

SEVEN

Teddy was sitting on the balcony having his usual cornflakes and coffee while reading the classic car magazine Brian had sent him from London.

He began to wonder why Jo was so long. She was usually back in an hour and three hours had passed. Then the telephone rang. It was the hospital to say that Jo had had a mild heart attack. She had been admitted onto ward six for observation and was asking for him.

Just then, George came from next door with the story of a large explosion on a yacht. "You can see the smoke from here, look," he said, but Teddy was trying to tell him that Jo was in hospital and he had to go. "I'll come with you," George said.

Both of them arrived at ward six to find Jo sitting up, having a cup of tea. She looked tired but wanted to tell her story of events while it was fresh in her mind. She also wanted Johnny Bellman and had asked one of the nurses to contact him. She described the people who had abducted her in detail and he passed the information on to Interpol.

The *Francina Marais* had been virtually destroyed as

fireworks and gas bottles had blown up, causing a huge fire which spread quickly, deep down in the heart of the boat.

The owner, his wife and two daughters had escaped, but a large woman, who was the cook, and three deckhands were rescued. One other man was found badly burned and dead.

A large amount of cocaine and other drugs were stored in a safe room, along with currency amounting to two million in mainly euros and American dollars. The catamaran was registered in San Francisco, USA, in the name of Vassily Freedman.

Johnny Bellman was looking into all sides of the story and found out that the drug cartel was well known by Interpol and they were closing in on some of the main operators. He also said that they were notorious for killing any people who caused them trouble.

Jo could not help feeling nervous as it could be 'third time lucky' for them. After all, she was seventy and not as strong as she used to be. The thought of two terrifying experiences and poor Ginger and Rhanan began to play on her mind.

Teddy decided that Jo was going to need more time to recuperate and it would be better to plan a world tour starting in France to stay with Suzanne and her family at the chateau. They could have a real distraction planning where to go and who to visit. The best hotels or staying with friends in Canada and America.

Money was no object and George and Gail would look after their apartment, and High Vista was doing really well in the hands of Cloe and Guido.

Brian was living in their house in London as he had let his properties and his classic car business was keeping him in England more. The more they thought about everything, the more the plan began to come together.

They made a list of all their friends and relations all around the world, sent letters to say they would like to visit and waited patiently for the replies.

The first reply they received was from Teddy's Aunty Maurine, his mother's sister in Canada. She was Teddy's favourite aunt when he was young and he really missed her when she married Ken Hammerman and moved to Canada after her first husband had died of a heart attack. They now lived not far from Lake Champlain.

Out of the fourteen letters sent there were two who had died, three were in homes due to medical reasons and two who had not replied. The remaining six were very exciting replies.

Jo's cousin living in New York was really pleased to receive their letter and would love to see them. The same with Teddy's old school friend, Horatio Frier, living in Sacramento, and Jo's distant relation, Velma, in San Francisco. John Adams, a retired sea captain living in New Zealand and two more cousins; sisters living in Singapore.

EIGHT

On the twentieth day of May they arrived in France. It was lovely and a joy to see the family in such a beautiful place and having such fun. Their three children: Haley, Christine and Sam, had settled in school and were coping with the French language very well. Teddy and Jo had done French O-level at school and most of that had been forgotten so the children enjoyed translating for them, especially when shopping in the market and ordering food in restaurants.

On the fourteenth of June they left from Charles De Gaul airport for New York. The flight was comfortable in first class to Kennedy Airport, and cousin Grant and his wife, Rosemarie, were there to meet them.

They lived in an old-fashioned house on Staten Island. Polished wooden floors were throughout the house. The large bathroom looked Victorian and everywhere was really charming. The weather was hot and humid, and even Teddy enjoyed a swim in their pool.

One day was spent in New York with the usual tourist visits to the Empire State building and lunch in the Empire Room. The shops on 42nd Street and a horse-drawn cab around

Central Park. Then going home on the Staten Island ferry past the Statue of Liberty on Liberty Island was a real treat.

After four enjoyable days they said their goodbyes, collected a small camper van from the airport and started their tour of America.

They headed for Boston and stayed in a camping ground near Wellesley, then spent two days just looking around, visiting Montpelier and then Lake Champlain, and found their way to Champlain and on to visit Aunty Maurine.

She was only about 4ft 11ins and full of energy despite being 87 years old. She loved taking them to all the local places of interest such as ski lodges and old Indian haunts.

One night there was a terrific storm. The lightning was constant, making everywhere pink, and the noise was tremendous. Jo seemed very nervous the next day and some of her old fears started to bother her again. Although Aunty Maurine and Ken would have loved them to stay longer, they understood the problem when they were told about the strain Jo had been through.

Next on the list was Buffalo and on to Niagara Falls. What a wonderful sight and feeling the fine spray was as they stood almost hypnotised by the great fall of water.

Jo said she was not feeling so good and would like to spend a few days in a hotel so they made their way to Newark Liberty International Airport where they left the camper van and boarded a plane to Chicago O'Hare Airport where Teddy had made a reservation at the Hilton Hotel.

The hotel was very large with all the amenities they needed. They took advantage of the tour offered to see the interesting parts of Chicago.

Jo felt so tired most of the time, but still remembered the beautiful architecture, and the big marble lions. She also managed to have a swim in the beautiful pool every day and tried to sound enthusiastic for Teddy's sake, but he could tell that his wife was struggling and the times he was awakened when she had the same nightmare about falling and falling, like the day at High Vista when she was thrown over the cliff.

He decided to speak to the hotel doctor and made an appointment for Jo to see him.The result was a prescription for some happy pills which helped a bit, but as Jo never knew when she would have the dream she still found it hard to sleep properly.

After a week with lots of rest and pills she told Teddy she was looking forward to going to see Kansas City which was next on the agenda.

NINE

Teddy was very good at organising things so when the flight from Chicago arrived in Kansas City, a camper van was there for them with a map of all the available campsites for miles around.

The plan was to head for the Badlands and then on to Yellowstone National Park. Top of the list was Old Faithful and the sulphur springs. Jo's silver bracelet was turned nearly black and the smell of eggs was not nice. Jo was feeling really tired again so they found a campsite to camp up for a day or two.

There were four camper vans among the tall trees and the other holiday travellers were making use of the tables and benches scattered around. The two campfires were burning brightly and one of the youngsters was strumming a guitar while his sister dang songs from films.

It was a beautiful starlit night. One young couple had a baby and there were six others who all seemed friendly and talkative.

"Have you seen that Native American man putting on a show?" an older woman named Joy asked Teddy.

"No, we have only just arrived, was it good?" he replied.

The rest of the evening was spent in animated tales of how the Chief, as he was known, seemed to hypnotise people without them realising it, but Joy's husband, Rob, said that he seemed to do good for people. "Stopped a man's back pain," he said.

Teddy told them about Jo having nightmares and how she was getting frightened to go to sleep. Rob and Joy both said that she should go to his show and see what happens.

The next night Teddy and Jo went with their two new friends to another campsite where about twenty people were gathered sitting at the picnic tables and some sitting on the ground near the fire. The scene looked magical, lighting up people's faces, then a chant came from a trail to the right and people began to clap as the Chief came into sight.

He spoke perfect English, which was very surprising to Teddy and Jo as he was adorned in full Indian headdress with beads and fringes on his soft white leather clothes.

Rob and Joy were the first to speak to him as they had met him a number of times. One or two other people spoke to him, then he began to dance and chant something indiscernible and moved towards a man on a bench, touching his shoulder with such force he nearly knocked him off the bench.

The woman with him laughed but the Chief took no notice and carried on with his chant and dance. Then he stood straight in front of Jo.

It was the first time she could see his face and eyes. Those eyes looked like a devil's eyes and before she could move his hand came up and pushed hard onto her forehead. Teddy immediately moved to her side but the Chief was moving away with his dance and chant. He then headed down the track where he had come from and vanished into the dark trees.

"Are you all right?" Teddy asked Jo. She nodded yes, then Rob and Joy came over, full of excitement.

"We told the Chief about your nightmares but we didn't think he would do anything about it as he hadn't met you before. You will be able to sleep now." The four of them headed for their campsite, said goodnight and went to bed. Jo had the best night's sleep since before the night of the storm at Aunty Maurine's.

They really enjoyed their visit to Yellowstone, seeing Old Faithful shooting up about every ninety minutes. They saw a herd of buffalo and the beautiful Yellowstone Falls. The little ground squirrels taking food out of their hands were charming.

Jo enjoyed finding postcards with all the animals and places they had seen to send back home to friends and family with a full report of their progress.

Teddy had noticed that Jo seemed more relaxed and free from worry since their stay in Yellowstone so they stayed for an extra two days before moving on to the Grand Canyon National Monument and the Grand Canyon itself, then Flagstaff and on to the impressive Hoover Dam, and then Las Vegas.

Las Vegas was exciting, with all the different casinos, with hundreds of happy people moving from slot machines to blackjack tables and playing Keno, which Teddy and Jo had never heard of before.

They started with 500 dollars for gambling money, which they nearly doubled on the first day, but cautiously they nearly gave it back playing blackjack the next day.

People told them to go through Death Valley during the early hours of the morning to avoid the relentless heat, so they went to bed early and slept until 2am, then ventured into Death Valley, aptly named as the heat was almost unbearable.

They were glad to reach Bishop, and after having such fun in Vegas they decided to head to Reno, stopping off on the way at Carson City.

TEN

Reno was fascinating. All lights and activity. The M.G.M., Caesars Palace and the Golden Nugget took their eye. "Lets book in at the M.G.M. for two nights," Teddy said and Jo agreed.

The first day went very quickly as they played on as many slot machines and tables as possible between eating fantastic food and drinking plenty of champagne. So when they eventually went to bed at two am they slept soundly.

They had never been to a casino before Vegas as they were always too busy building up their business and looking after the children, so Vegas and Reno held a real fascination but their conservative upbringing was always there to stop them going too far into gambling.

It was the evening of the second day that they were attracted by a large wedding party having fun. "Who's wedding is it?" Jo asked an excited couple standing next to them."

"Gordon Grey, one of the richest people in San Francisco, who has married a beautiful and wealthy Russian girl called Isabella Miscove. They make a very handsome couple, don't you think?"

"Teddy, it's her." Jo was pulling at Teddy's arm and leading him towards the group of people with the most strikingly beautiful bride.

"Alo," Jo said, mimicking the voice in Spain when she had caught Jo's attention. "And this gorgeous hunk must be your new husband. Congratulations, you make a lovely couple," She said, taking Gordon's hand. "How is your sister, Isy?"

Isy looked pale and lost for words. "You have just missed them. She and Isy's father had to leave early to attend to some business in Mexico." Gordon told them.

"Well, it's lovely bumping into you like this but we must not keep you from your guests; have a lovely honeymoon and a happy life ahead, bye for now." And they left smiling at them.

"What was that all about?" Teddy asked. "Are you sure she is the person you saw in Fuengirola; part of the family who abducted you and tried to kill you?"

"Didn't you see the look of shock on her face?" Jo said. "Let's leave for Sacramento now. Your friend is on the internet and we can get in touch with Johnny and tell him about Isy Grey. You go and get our case from the room, while I go to the ladies and I will get the camper van from the garage and meet you at the front."

Isy was hurrying to reach Jo and stood in front of her. "Mrs Jensen, please, I would like to talk to you. I am so sorry about all the things that happened in the past." She carried on, "I have escaped from the past and Gordon does not know anything about that. My father arranged for our name to be changed and bought another yacht, then carried on to South America as usual. I knew I had to change my life and my cousins in San Francisco were willing to help me and so I met Gordon. So please, please, can you forget the past. I will give you money if you like."

Gordon was heading towards them so Jo smiled. "I can see my wife is pleased to see you again. Where did you meet the Moscove family?"

"In Spain," Jo answered, "and on that beautiful yacht."

"Oh yes, *Cave Lady*," he answered. "She is beautiful, but I have a much bigger and more beautiful yacht so Isy will feel at home. You are most welcome to visit when we get back. She is in the marina. You can't miss her, she is named *Isabella*," he said as he looked lovingly at his wife.

"Thanks," Jo said. "We will meet again but now I must go as Teddy will be missing me."

They headed for Sacramento after Teddy had been in touch with his old school friend, Horatio Frier, who said it did not matter how late they arrived as he was writing a book and did most of his work at night. Hatty, as he was known, was only too pleased to send an email to Johnny Bellman telling him of the new name of the Moscove family and their new yacht, *Cave Lady*.

Jo told Teddy all that Isy had said. She also told him that she thought Isy was genuinely sorry so Jo was not going to mention her name.

"Don't be silly," Teddy retorted. "She is part of that family who tried to kill you not once but twice, so don't be taken in by a sob story."

"Well, let's just see what happens," Jo said, and with that they went to sleep.

ELEVEN

Hatty was not at all like Jo had imagined him. He was over six feet tall and very fat. His bald head was shiny and he had an enormous ginger beard. He and Teddy were remembering their days at school and spending holidays camping and training in Wales.

"I'm not usually up until midday but today I have an appointment with a friend of mine at Davis University. He's a prof in marine biology and is helping me with some details I need for my latest book. Why don't you come with me? You could look around the university while I do some work, which shouldn't take more than two hours, then we could have lunch wherever and, make a day of it."

It didn't take long before Teddy and Jo found out that Hatty was quite a well-known celebrity. Evidently he had written six books and received a prize for literature from the university.

They wandered around the campus and then into Davis where they met Hatty for lunch at one of the small cafes, where they had pancakes and maple syrup, which was a change from their usual food but very enjoyable. Hatty took them for a ride to Dixon, Woodland and El Macero and then back to

Sacramento to the Pepper Mill for a great steak. Altogether a lovely enjoyable day.

The next morning Teddy and Jo were awakened with the sound of Hatty singing *Jerusalem* while cooking very thin bacon to a lovely crisp.

"How do you like your bacon – soggy or crisp?" he yelled up the stairs. "I've poached the eggs as I remembered how you like them Ted." The waft of fresh coffee seemed to fill the house. "Good morning you two, sleep well?" he enquired. "Now," he went on, "I have to go away tomorrow for two weeks to a book fair in Washington and then on to Canada to Montreal for another. You are welcome to stay here so I will give you a key so that you can come and go as you please. Keep the key in case you are over here in the future as well."

The doorbell rang. "That's my tickets being delivered by courier." Hatty came back clutching his tickets and flight plan with a happy look on his face.

"There's one thing good about having a bestseller and an understanding agent," he said. "One travels first class, staying at the best hotels, usually in a suit with all the facilities, not just a room, and chauffeur driven wherever you fancy going. It's a bit of a 'B' having to sign books for about two hours at a time. But a small price to pay.

"Oh, I nearly forgot, I have the Happy Home Agency team come in once a month to clean and they are due tomorrow. They have their own key, so if you can go out for about four hours and let them get on with it. Just leave your washing on your bed and they will do everything.

"Now, I will be picked up at seven am in good time for my flight at 9:30am. I'm already packed so I suggest that we go to Old Sacramento. I think you will like to see where the Pony Express riders came in after crossing America with the mail. They were the most successful postal service ever. Never lost anything."

Hatty was right; Old Sacramento with its boardwalks, old fashioned restaurants, shops and the old trains were all really interesting. There is a beautiful bronze pony express rider on his horse that Jo had to photograph and buy postcards to send to Brian and Suzanne and friends.

They sat outside at the end of the street, eating beef burgers while watching some cowboys doing amazing things with lassoes and very long whips. Then as the sun went down they all sang cowboy songs and yodled. The end to a perfect day.

TWELVE

The next morning they were awake at eight o'clock so they had a quick breakfast and were gone by nine to avoid the Happy Home team. They spent the day visiting the capitol building. The guides took parties of about ten people around and explained all about the history of the past one hundred years. All very interesting.

After two more days just lounging around and watching TV they decided to go to San Francisco and find a hotel to stay in for three or four days, then return to Hatty's.

The weather was beautiful when they arrived in Fisherman's Wharf. Such an interesting place but so crowded. They bought a coffee and cake then found a table for four where one girl was drinking orange juice, so asked her if she minded if they joined her.

She looked startled and looked around nervously, then she nodded and smiled. "You are Mr and Mrs Jensen," she said quietly. "I shouldn't be seen with you. I'm Isy's friend and know that you are in grave danger. I went on board *Isabella* just before they left to help her unpack and she showed me around, then some other friends arrived and she had to meet them so she asked me to take some of her things to a big closet on the upper deck. While I was there I heard Gordon talking to a man about getting rid of two people while they were away. The named people were Teddy and Jo Jensen and 'Isy must not suspect anything'.

"Gordon is just as bad as all her family. Isy thinks she is safe but cousins who helped her were in on it the whole time, pretending to be her friends. I picked up one of the photos left on the table; look." she said as she took a small print out of her handbag.

It was a picture taken at the casino when Teddy and Jo had first met Isy and Gordon. "I heard your names and also heard Gordon say, 'See it's done before we get back. The money will be in the usual place.'

"The two men left and I came out of the closet and could see this picture left on the table. I wanted to tell Isy but she is infatuated by Gordon and would not believe me, and she would tell him and I would then be on the hit list, so I am going to Singapore with my brother to stay with our family and hope not to see the Moscoves ever again. We fly out tomorrow. There's my brother now. Good luck," she said, rising from the table as she waved to a tall good-looking man and they walked away together.

"My God, what do you think of that?"

Teddy looked at Jo, "I think we had better go back to Hatty's place and stay there until we decide what to do."

Their lovely enjoyable holiday had turned into a nightmare. "What if we have been seen? What if they know our camper van and follow us to Hatty's?"

They left San Francisco nervously, keeping a lookout for any signs of being followed.

THIRTEEN

Two weeks to the day, Hatty arrived back at around six in the evening, full of exuberance. The whole trip had been very successful and he had signed a contract to have one of his books made into a film, but he was exhausted as he had had very little sleep for the last two days.

"This is one night I will not be up to writing," he said with a yawn. "You will have to excuse me but if I don't go to bed I will collapse in a heap. Tomorrow you can tell me what you've been up to while I've been away."

Teddy and Jo stayed up watching a film on TV which was very exciting about the war and helped keep their minds occupied until they went to bed.

They were awakened with, "Jerusalem, Jerusalem," Hatty's lovely deep voice rang out. Somehow it made them feel happier and Hatty had made bacon and eggs with corn cobs and fresh coffee, and the whole house felt comfortable again.

"Well, come on you two, tell me what you have been up to in the last two weeks. You seem too glum to be on holiday." Teddy and Jo told him the whole story from start to finish and asked him what he would do.

"What a wonderful story. I feel another bestseller coming on."

Hatty seemed excited with the whole idea of writing another book.

Teddy was trying to contain his annoyance. "Well, if we are killed this next week feel free to write the 'Jensen story', but in the meantime we were hoping for some sensible advice on how to avoid death."

Hatty looked at Jo's strained face and realised how worried she was, "Sorry," he said. "This will take some thought. Have you told your friend in Spain, Johnny Bellman?"

They rang Johnny, who sounded most concerned and suggested that they should return to Fuengirola where they could be protected.

"But isn't that the way these horrible people could trace us?" Jo said.

Hatty raised his hand and then his finger. "I know someone who can help with that," he said. "My friend, Scotty, is a pilot with his own plane who does charter flights for the rich and famous. He tells the airline to reserve first class seats, in your case for two celebrities, no names mentioned, then you arrive, show your passports, pay for your flight and go on your way without any bother. How does that sound?"

They both nodded 'yes' and Hatty dialled a number and asked to speak to Hamish McVay. "Hi Scotty, Hatty here. I have two celebs who need to get a flight from the US to Malaga, Spain, as soon as possible. Pick up at Sacramento. They could go from Chicago depending on the first flights available. You do your magic and let me know ASAP. Thanks, Scotty, you're the best," and he rang off, turning to them with his usual grin. "A bit expensive but you can afford it."

About an hour later the call came in. Scotty would be at Sacramento airport tomorrow at 9am. Flight at nine thirty to Newark, New Jersey for a flight at ten thirty the next day to Malaga, Spain.

FOURTEEN

The camper van was emptied and cleaned and two big cases were put into the under stairs closet at Hatty's, so they only had a holdall each to take with them. "Come on, come on." Hatty had his serious side and insisted he was coming with them to introduce them to Scotty.

It was 8am when they arrived at the reception desk and Hatty said, "Hamish McVay's flight passengers," to a smart young man who took one look at Hatty and said.

"Mr Frier, good morning, nice to see you," and beckoned them all through the gate. They sat in a very comfortable lounge with a pretty blonde girl pouring coffee for them.

"Mr McVay is doing the flight plan and will be ready at nine," she said with a smile.

An extremely smart man came towards them. "Hatty, you old devil, good to see you." He and Hatty had a big hug, then Hatty introduced them and Linda took them to a check in where they bought two tickets and before they realised they were on board a beautiful Learjet.

"This is the way to travel," Teddy mused with a grin as another pretty blonde girl called Tara was pouring champagne and another smart young man introduced himself as the co-pilot, James Greer.

It all went so smoothly that when they were in-flight they suddenly realised that they had not said cheerio to Hatty. "Never mind, we will obviously be seeing him again if he writes that book he was so excited about."

They really enjoyed their special flight with lots of good champagne and a beautifully prepared meal of seafood, finishing with crème brûlée, and instead of a film they tuned into the flight channel, which was very interesting. They felt that the whole experience was something they would always remember.

Then suddenly jet lag hit them as Tara was taking them to the first class lounge for their onward flight to Malaga, so they slept for most of the way and were soon landing in Spain where George and Gail were at the airport to meet them.

"We are really glad that you have cut short your world tour," Gail said. "Things are a bit of a pickle at High Vista. Cloe is pregnant with twins and had to go into hospital with complications, so poor Guido is in a panic and struggling. He has taken on more staff but he is worried that when the twins arrive he will not be able to cope."

They were soon back at the apartment in Fuengirola and the first thing they did was call Johnny Bellman to let him know that they were back, and then they made their way up to High Vista.

It all looked the same: very pretty, with children splashing around in the pool and Guido was smiling and talking to some customers when he noticed them.

"How is Cloe?" Jo asked.

"The bambinos will be arriving later today," he said. "She is to have a cesarean." Teddy and Jo assured him that they would take over until all was well with Cloe and the little ones.

It felt really good to be back and to have something to do. Johnny, his family and Philippo came to see them and it seemed that they had not been away.

High Vista had its local friends with families who had made it their favourite place to have fun and eat out, and bookings were selling well for parties up to the new year.

"It looks as if we are out of retirement for a while." Teddy laughed. Johnny and Philippo wanted a serious word and they produced two photographs: one of an older man, rougher looking, and the other of a smart man about forty-ish.

"Have you ever seen these two anywhere?" Johnny asked. Teddy and Jo had a good look at both the pictures and shook their heads to say no, when one of the Spanish waiters noticed the picture of the older man and asked why they had a picture of his father.

They sat down at a table and asked him why his father was in San Francisco. Evidently he worked on private yachts and was often there. Only last week he had spoken to him and was told that the yacht he worked on was going into dry dock for about three months for a complete overhaul, so he would be out of a job and was looking for temporary work. He had good references and also a retainer so then he would go back to work for the same family.

The San Francisco police were hot on the case and confirmed the waiter's story so he was eliminated from further inquiries. So it was the smart younger man who was the suspected assassin.

High Vista was running smoothly. The chef and staff were very efficient so Jo was not overworked and Teddy decided that he and Jo would not go individually but always be together for security.

They soon recognised the local regulars and Guido came for about two hours a day just to have a break from the twin boys, who were doing well, as was Cloe, so he was all full of enthusiasm.

It was during a very busy time catering for an eightieth birthday party when Jo noticed a big bald man with a large ginger beard coming towards the pool. "Hatty," she yelled. They had a big hug. "What are you doing here? How wonderful to see you." She waved for Teddy to come over.

"Good to see you," Teddy said. "We will be about half an hour so have something to eat and drink then we will be free to go home. Help yourself at the buffet or ask Guido for anything you want."

Hatty seemed very happy to sit and look around while eating half a chicken with all the trimmings, washed down with a bottle of Spanish white.

The were soon back at the apartment and Hatty settled in, they then found out why he had come to see them. He said that three days after Teddy and Jo left, the police had brought two photos and asked if they recognised either of the two men.

The next day a smart man had knocked on his door and introduced himself as Patrick O'Neil. He asked Hatty if he would sign six books for him as he and his wife Mary had enjoyed reading them so much.

Hatty recognised him immediately from one of the photos, so he autographed the books and pretended to be unconcerned but very busy when his secretary, Linda Jones, arrived to work on his next book. Linda and her husband, Aled, always stayed to look after the place when Hatty was on his book tours. Hatty had a TV interview in London and another book fair in Edinburgh so decided to make a detour to Spain to see them, especially as he wanted to see High Vista for himself; he was very keen to start the new book about the Jensens.

The next day they took Hatty to Fuengirola to show him their favourite places. He had a little book which he kept on getting out and writing notes. "All to jog my memory when I get home," he said with his usual grin.

"Let's go back to High Vista to finish the day off," Teddy suggested.

"Good idea, then you can fill me in on the events that happened there, where and when." Hatty was interrupted by Teddy shaking his head violently, so he stopped talking and Teddy changed the subject tactfully as they were walking along the sea front and the sand sculptures were exceptionally good.

Later at High Vista, Hatty exuded, "I'm not surprised this place is so popular. This is excellent paella, and it is such a beautiful setting and very romantic under the stars on a warm night."

Some friends sat at the next table and Jo excused herself to go and talk to them so Teddy took the opportunity to quickly tell Hatty not to mention anything about when Jo was thrown over the cliff. He did not want her returning to the nervous state she had been in for months before she had seen the Chief in Yellowstone. Hatty understood and made a note in his little book.

The next day Hatty had to leave for London, but said he would be back soon.

FIFTEEN

Apart from one wet day the weather was beautiful and the restaurant was nicely busy. Cloe was getting back her energy and brought the twins up to High Vista every day. They were named Arrin and Bruno, A and B, first and second born. Fortunately they looked different. Arrin was smaller than his brother Bruno, so they were easily distinguishable.

Time seemed to race by and it was nearly two weeks since Hatty had left when they were awakened by the doorbell at 4.30am. Teddy put the lights on and went cautiously to the door and looked through the small peephole where he could see Johnny.

"Come in, what a time to be calling. It had better be a good reason."

Johnny said that he had an email from the international police that the assassin was travelling under the name of Chelso Magetti and had arrived in Spain, so Fuengirola police were instructed to notify Teddy and Jo immediately, and to advise them to wear body protectors whenever they went out. "So I have brought you two," he said.

"I'm going to ask Hatty to come back, as he will be able to identify him if he turns up here," Teddy said.

Jo made fresh coffee and they sat and discussed the safest way to deal with the situation.

First, ring Johnny ten minutes before leaving the apartment. Second, always wear the body protectors. Third, each to carry pepper spray and a loud screecher alarm, and always be alert to their surroundings. Make sure the house alarm is switched on when they go to bed and when they go out, and try not to get into a routine of going out and coming in at the same time each day. Also check the car at all times before getting into it.

Johnny told them what to look for, and if there was anything that looked suspicious, get away from it and ring him.

By now it was 5.15am and Teddy and Jo were wide awake, and Johnny was ready to go home and go to sleep as he had had a busy night.

Teddy rang Hatty and told him the news, and asked him if he could come back for a couple of weeks. Hatty seemed very pleased to have a holiday in Fuengirola after a hectic two weeks dealing with his book life.

The checklist became part of daily life, just taking up more time, and although irritating they thought it was a small price to pay to be safe.

Hatty arrived and spent more time on his own getting to know the place and surrounding areas but always finished up at High Vista in the evening for a meal and to talk about the day. He was very observant of everything, and his little book had already been replaced with a new one.

SIXTEEN

"Magetti, table for two." Guido seated them and handed them the menus. Hatty recognised him as Patrick O'Neil.

"Looks like it's game on at last." Hatty sounded excited. Jo went over to another table where two ladies were eating. They were police women blending in and they had noticed the man too so had already sent the message to Johnny.

Hatty made the first move. "Hello, Mr O'Neil, fancy seeing you here. And this must be Mary, your wife." He smiled at the attractive woman.

"No, you are mistaken," she said. "This is Chelso Magetti and I am Christine. We met on board, we're just friends."

Then Johnny and Nico walked up and produced a photo of the same man named Vladimir Cheleski. "Mr Cheleski, we have been looking for you," Johnny said, and then Jo joined in.

"Mr Magetti, I am the person you are looking for to kill."

"And I am the other person you are looking for to kill." said Teddy. By now Christine was looking very concerned and stood up from the table, but before she could move away Magetti pulled a knife from his pocket, and with one arm around her shoulders pressed the knife against her neck.

"Move away," he said menacingly, "or I will kill her." But before he could do anything else Hatty's big hand grasped the knife while his other hand pressed hard on the pressure point on Magetti's neck. All over in a second, Jo grabbed Christine's arm and took her to a chair at another table while Nico handcuffed the assassin.

Some people at the next table were looking very worried. "Very amateur dramatics." Guido laughed and carried on as though nothing had happened while offering them the dessert menu. The two police women led Magetti away into the police car, out of sight.

Christine was very shocked but Guido was so charming and so casual with her that she began to settle down. "Just think what a story you will be able to tell your friends when you get back home," Hatty said, "and if you give me permission I will write you into the book all about the Jensens. It's a good ending to finish with don't you think?"

Christine told them how she and Magetti had become friends on board, but Magetti was travelling with another man called Emmit and she thought she saw him just before they arrived at High Vista. Johnny seemed very interested in finding out all about him and Christine was able to give a good description, especially about a large tattoo on his left hand and arm. It was a red and black snake, which she found scary, and she had noticed that every time she was with Magetti he had kept out of sight but was always in the background.

Christine had lost her husband four years earlier and had decided to go on a cruise with her friend, Joan. Joan had met a man she liked as soon as they boarded the ship, so Christine was on her own right from the start and that was when Magetti had noticed her. They liked playing cards and dancing and Christine thought he was a gentleman on his own, whose wife had died.

The ship had docked in Gibraltar for two days, so they decided to take a coach trip to Fuengirola to see the fair, and stay there for one night, then catch the coach back the following day.

"I'm glad I found out what he was really like before things progressed too seriously," she said.

Teddy invited her to join them, with Hatty, as they were all ready to eat, and afterwards they took her back to the hotel she was booked into and made sure she was happy changing into another room to feel safe.

Back at High Vista, things were carrying on as usual, with no one having any idea of what happened earlier. "We didn't know that you were ready for what happened" Jo said to Guido.

"Hatty put me in the picture, and he also showed me the photo of the man to look out for so I was ready when I saw him arriving, but the main plan was to make sure that everyone was safe and as little disruption as possible to the other people in the restaurant," he said.

Apart from the one table next to the activity, no one had noticed anything, so everything carried on as usual, mainly down to Guido's nonchalant carefree attitude and Conny and Ava, not dressed in police uniform, played a big part in removing the handcuffed man without drawing attention to him.

SEVENTEEN

Back at the apartment they had a whiskey each and talked about the events of the day.

"Hatty, you were amazing; how you managed to disarm whatever his name is, and I think you might have saved Christine's life. Where did you learn what to do?" Jo said.

They were told that when he was at university he had decided that he wanted to be a writer, so he joined the marines for five years as he thought he would gain more things through experience to write about. He then moved to a firm who supplied bodyguards for famous people and politicians for which he had to have thorough training. "I was very fit in those days," he said with his usual grin. "And I certainly gained lots of experiences of life."

"I married my lovely Georgina and we had a baby girl we called Jessica. Georgy was pregnant again when she was killed in a car crash. At the time I was contracted for another two years as a bodyguard so Georgina's parents looked after Jess in Sacramento. Now she is happily married with two children and she and her husband are doctors. I see them regularly and I have set up a uni fund for the two little ones."

"Well I didn't know all that; you never mentioned anything at all about the things you were doing except your writing, and even then you never said how well you were doing," Teddy said.

Hatty shrugged with his usual grin, but a thoughtful faraway look was in his eyes. "That reminds me, I really do have to go home. I have been away too long as I have an important meeting to attend next week and Jess has a birthday coming up on the 4th November, so I will contact my friend, Scotty, and see if he is available. I'm lucky I am employed by him as a bodyguard when he needs one so I can usually hitch a lift."

Scotty was on his way to Ireland with a hen party from America. He then had to go to New York to pick up a party of bankers going to a conference in San Francisco so that he could divert to Malaga to pick up Hatty in good time for him to be back for Jess's birthday.

Jo suggested that as he had a couple of days before the flight with Scotty, that they could go to the fair.

October in Fuengirola is an exciting time as the big annual fair takes place. Beautiful Spanish horses with ladies sitting sideways behind the men parade the streets in colourful costumes.

They congregate at the large fairground where they move from one bar to another, and where anyone can talk to them and pat the beautiful animals. Everyone is friendly and there is such an atmosphere of fun and camaraderie with the flamenco music sounding out everywhere. Teddy, Jo and Hatty spent the two days taking in the traditions of the local people. Even the young family members were dressed immaculately.

They recognised their two police guards, Conny and Ava, taking it in turns to blend in and they also noticed a Spanish-looking man in a red shirt, but there was something different as whenever he met another similarly dressed man there was no acknowledgement and he always moved away quickly, whereas others always chatted.

Conny and Ava had also noticed him and notified Johnny so there was an immediate check taking place. He was a shady character called Emmit Van Doran from America, and had arrived on the same cruise ship as Chelso Magetti.

Jo began to feel uneasy so they headed back to High Vista especially as Johnny and Nico had decided to arrest him, Emmit Van Doran as the San Francisco police had asked for him to be returned to the US to face charges on two accounts of murder. Also, the dark clouds could be seen rolling down the distant mountains looking ominously like a big storm coming.

They took Hatty to the station as he went in his way to meet up with Scotty for the lift home.

They had a restless night with thunder and lightning overhead for about an hour. The next morning there were palm branches and rubbish littering the beautiful garden everywhere. Jo wanted to go up to High Vista early to see if everything was alright.

"What a mess!" Jo exclaimed. The pool was covered with leaves and pieces of paper. Chairs and tables were overturned and rubbish everywhere. They set about clearing the pool and Guido tidied up the main dining area. The chef was preparing the menu and cooking beef while the cook planned her dishes.

Some of the lights around the pool were broken and had to be replaced, but things were back to normal just in time for lunch and people began to trickle in as usual, and all was well.

EIGHTEEN

"Looks like we are a retired couple again," Teddy laughed. They were soon back in their old routine: going out with friends, playing bridge, visiting vineyards on their coach trips and entertaining friends and relations from England.

Johnny told them that they had failed to arrest Emmit Van Doran but felt that he was no longer a threat as he had supposedly been seen in Brazil and the American police were dealing with him.

George and Gail were special friends and they all liked to meet up at the coffee shop in the gated community and just chat.

It was Friday the thirteenth, not that anyone noticed, when they were about to leave the apartment to meet at the coffee shop as usual when the telephone rang. It was Suzannah, so Jo told Teddy to go on and she would be there in a few minutes. About five minutes later she finished the call and hurried out, making sure the door closed behind her, and as she turned towards the stairway she suddenly saw the familiar face of Emmit Van Doran holding a pistol straight at her. She froze, then raised her left hand with her bag, as if trying to protect herself.

He fired the gun, but she felt nothing as she fell to the floor with blood pouring profusely from her arm and her mouth.

There were two armed security guards who heard the gun go off and shouted as Emmit turned to fire at the first who fell, but his friend fired at Emmit at the same time. His aim was good and Emmit fell behind the wall.

For a moment all was quiet, then people began to appear from all areas. George and Teddy told Grace to stay in the cafe while they ran across to the second courtyard, where a woman yelled for someone to call the Guarda and paramedics as she was trying to stem the blood from the guard on the ground, while the second guard was cautiously making his way up to the stairwell and up the corridor where Jo lay. He saw Emmit and noted that he was dead, then looked at Jo covered in blood but still breathing and beginning to move. Teddy and George were not far behind and helped her to sit up, and tried to hold a clean handkerchief against the wound on her ear. The paramedics were soon there and Jo was taken to the hospital again.

She had seen Emmit and felt that he would not be a problem anymore.

Apart from having a shattered wisdom tooth removed and three stitches on her right ear, her arm was bound and she was given painkillers by injection and sent home with a box of pills and told to rest for a few days.

They all kept telling her how lucky she had been. She knew she was but at that moment it didn't feel much like luck.

NINETEEN

Three times Jo had narrowly missed death and each time she had recovered well. Seeing Emmit dead was always on her mind, as though now he was gone she felt free. Surely now Teddy and she could get on with normal life. She had time to reflect on the past three years and wondered where the beautiful Isy was and if she was safe. The *Isabella* had not returned to San Francisco and was last seen in Hong Kong with the *Cave Lady* there too.

Jo had always looked forward to Christmas and Alan and Suzannah had invited them to the chateau and they were looking forward to seeing their grandchildren again.

Jo's wounds healed quickly, and apart from having what looked like a dimple on her left cheek, she looked normal. The life at High Vista was always exciting, with party time up to the new year after which Cloe and Guido had chosen to close for six weeks to update the decor and spend time with their families so that they could see the twins before they grew out of the baby stage.

"Well, Mrs Jensen, I hardly dare say we are officially retired," Teddy said. "And we can visit our relations and friends and perhaps we could visit our elderly relations, the two sisters in Hong Kong and Hatty in Sacramento."

"Forget the two sisters, but, Hatty, yes," she replied. The thought of *Cave Lady* and *Isabella* being in Hong Kong was not a welcoming thought, but Hatty would be great and they would be able to see San Francisco again and explore the California coastline before they were too old to enjoy things.

Just before Christmas, when they were about to leave for France, a parcel arrived. It contained a dozen books. *The Jensen Story,* by Horatio Frier.

This book is printed on paper from sustainable sources managed under the Forest Stewardship Council (FSC) scheme.

It has been printed in the UK to reduce transportation miles and their impact upon the environment.

For every new title that Troubador publishes, we plant a tree to offset CO_2, partnering with the More Trees scheme.

For more about how Troubador offsets its environmental impact, see www.troubador.co.uk/sustainability-and-community